TWO MYSTE

FOR YOU TO SOLVE!

Match Wits With Detective Tommy Preston

The Monkey's Clue
The Stolen Sapphire

By Edward D. Hoch

With Illustrations by Tien Ho

inkpot books

GROSSET & DUNLAP

A FILMWAYS COMPANY

Publishers • New York

Library of Congress catalog card number: 78-58882
ISBN: 0-448-16367-5 (Paperback Edition)
ISBN: 0-448-13477-6 (Library Edition)
Published simultaneously in Canada
Printed in the United States of America

For Mary Sullivan

CONTENTS

THE MONKEY'S CLUE

Every afternoon at four o'clock, after he'd returned home from school, Tommy Preston helped his father, the zoo keeper, feed the animals. It was a job he especially liked, but on this particular Wednesday afternoon in May, he was content to turn it over to his older sister, Sandy.

"Just where do you think you're going?" she asked.

"Over to the monkey lab," he replied. "You'll feed them for me, won't you, sis?"

"You hang around that monkey lab long enough and they'll put you in one of the cages," she said. But she took the pail of fish from him, as he'd known she would. Feeding the seals was one thing she especially enjoyed.

Tommy Preston had just turned thirteen that spring. He was shorter than most of the other boys in his

class and maybe that was why he didn't play football and baseball as much as they did. Most of the time he was content to be around the zoo with his father and sister, though when his best friend, Mitch Grady, came to take him off on some adventure, he was always willing to go.

That was how he'd learned about the monkey lab in the first place. Mitch had seen a story in the newspaper about attempts to communicate with animals, and he'd shown it to Tommy.

"Wouldn't it be great if we could talk to all the animals in your father's zoo?" he'd asked.

"I think that's a long way from happening, Mitch." Nevertheless, the story interested him.

On their first visit to the lab, Tommy and Mitch struck up a friendship with Nora Thayer, the bright young lab assistant who was helping train the chimps. Though she was out of college and a good ten years older than the boys, she enjoyed showing them around the lab and answering their questions about the experiments.

"You see this display?" she asked, pointing to a board of sixty-four symbols on the wall of the chimpanzee's cage. "We've trained Max, the chimp, to communicate with us by pressing the right symbols in order. Look here."

With only a little urging, Max ambled up to the board and pressed three of the big square buttons.

"What's he saying?" Mitch Grady asked.

"Those symbols mean *Max want food,* and I reward him by pressing this button at my side, which drops food into his tray. You can see your talks with him must be fairly simple, but he does understand and respond."

The chimp hit four more buttons and she translated

for them. "*Max want play tree.* He wants to go climb the monkey tree."

If there was any one thing at the lab that fascinated Tommy as much as the trained chimp, it was definitely the monkey-puzzle tree just outside the back door of the lab. The evergreen, native to Chile, was called a monkey puzzle because, it was said, the branches were so twisted and prickly that even a monkey would have trouble climbing it.

Tommy liked to stand and stare at the monkey puzzle, but he hadn't risked climbing it since that first day, when he tore his shirt on it. Max was one monkey who wasn't discouraged by the puzzle, though. The tree's edible nuts were too great a temptation, and he would scurry up the trunk at the first opportunity. Sometimes he would signal his desire on the machine: *Max want play tree.*

This day, having arranged for Sandy to help his father with the animals, Tommy hurried off to meet Mitch for their visit to the lab. Actually it was on a college campus not far from the zoo, in a little one-story building separated from the others.

Nora Thayer seemed especially pleased to see them when they arrived. "I'm so glad you're here," she said. "I hate being alone."

"Max is with you," Tommy pointed out, going over to the cage to say hello. He set down a library book Mitch had returned to him.

"Well, yes, but it's not the same. Even though I can talk to him on the machine, it's not like having another person here." She glanced around and lowered her voice. "Frankly, I'm a bit frightened. Someone's been prowling around at night, trying to break in here, and with Professor Blake on vacation, I'm all alone."

"Why would anyone want to break in?" Tommy asked.

"Some of the research we've done here — with Max and with other animals — is extremely valuable. Many people would like to steal our records."

"Do you know who?"

"It would have to be someone who's familiar with our work here. I——"

Before she could say more, Max interrupted with his familiar message. *Max want play tree.*

Nora pressed the buttons on her keyboard to light up a return message. *Max want food first?*

No. Max want play tree.

"Oh, very well," she decided. She released the bar on the back door of his cage and they watched the chimp scurry across the yard to the monkey-puzzle tree.

"Look at him climb that thing!" Mitch exclaimed. "It's not a puzzle to him!"

Tommy had been thinking about something on his last couple of visits, and now he got up the courage to ask. "Nora, could I talk to Max on the machine, do you think?"

"Sure, Tommy. After he comes back inside."

She showed him how to work the sixty-four buttons with the symbols. "You see, there are symbols for *Max*, *Nora*, and *Professor*, because we're the only two who communicate regularly with him. The rest of the symbols are for common verbs like *want*, *eat*, *play*, and *sleep*, and nouns like *tree*, *cage*, *food*, *water*, and *bed*. You simply punch the buttons in order, as you've seen me do, and the symbols light up inside the cage."

Tommy was about to try it when they were interrupted by the arrival of a bearded graduate student named Michael Bush. He often stopped by the monkey lab when Tommy was there, and seemed to be especially fond of Nora.

"Hi, kids," he greeted them. "How's Max today?"

Nora did not seem pleased to see him. "He's up the tree," she replied.

"Where's the boss?"

"If you mean Professor Blake, he's away on business," she answered coldly. "If you'll excuse me, I have work to do."

But Michael Bush didn't leave at once. He strolled around the lab, glancing at the monkey cage and at some of the papers on Nora's desk, until finally she said, "You know those reports are confidential. Please leave now."

"Sure," he said with a smile. "I didn't mean any harm."

After he'd gone, Tommy asked, "Is he the one that's been sneaking around?"

Nora thought about it. "I don't know, Tommy."

They went out to the puzzle tree then, and coaxed Max down from the tangled branches. When he was back in his cage, Tommy tried talking to him, using the symbols. Max regarded him with some interest, but did not immediately respond.

"If you had a banana, he'd answer you," Mitch suggested.

"Try one," Nora said, handing Tommy a banana.

Max want banana? Tommy asked.

Yes, was the reply.

"My dad should have one of these over at the zoo," Tommy said.

"It takes months of training for the simplest communication," Nora assured him. "And I doubt if it would work with any animals other than chimpanzees. There have been experiments in communication with dolphins, but those use a different technique."

It was almost dinner time and Tommy knew his folks would be expecting him home. As he and Mitch were leaving, Nora had another visitor. This one was Sam Young, a curly-haired man who was a graduate student like Michael Bush. It was obvious that Nora liked Sam a good deal more than she did Michael.

He said hello to Tommy and Mitch and then turned to Nora. "I was driving by earlier and I saw Bush coming out. Is he still bothering you?"

"Oh, he's always hanging around," Nora said. "I'm tired of seeing him."

"Are you alone again?"

She nodded. "It's confidential, but Professor Blake is in Boston, seeing about a position at one of the big universities there. If he leaves, I might be placed in charge of the lab here."

"I thought he was happy here."

"He is, and he'd hate to abandon all the work he's done with Max. His research here is the property of the university, of course. But it's a great opportunity for him. The Boston program is funded by a private corporation dedicated to research into animal intelligence."

Sam Young was still with Nora when the boys left for home, and Mitch said, "She really likes him, huh?"

"I guess so," Tommy agreed. "A lot better than that Bush fellow, anyway."

It was later that evening, almost bedtime, when Tommy realized he'd left his library book at the monkey lab. He knew he'd need it the next day at school, and the lab was never open before noon. Looking out his upstairs window, he could just make out the lights of the lab building through the trees. That meant Nora was working late.

"Where do you think you're going?" Tommy's mother asked as he came downstairs and headed for the front door.

"Just over to the monkey lab, Mom. I forgot a library book."

"I don't like you out this late at night."

"It's only two blocks away. I'll be back in five minutes."

"Oh, all right, but be careful."

Tommy ran all the way, trotting along the sidewalk under the line of street lights. There was little traffic around the campus, and when he reached the lab building Nora's car was the only one in a parking space. He rang the bell and waited, but she didn't come.

Finally he went around the side to knock on the window, and that was when he saw her. She was sprawled on the floor just inside the door, as if she'd fainted. But one glance at the rest of the room told Tommy it was more than that. Papers had been pulled from the desks and filing cabinet, and several loose wires dangled from the monkey-communication panel. Max, sensing Tommy's presence, was pounding on the bars of his cage.

There was no way to get inside without breaking a window, and Tommy was afraid that might damage important evidence. Hoping that Nora wasn't badly hurt, he ran home and called the police.

Nora had a bump on the head, but she was all right otherwise. Shortly after dark the bell had rung, but when she went to the door of the lab building, no one was there. Sticking her head out to peer around, she'd been hit with a blunt instrument of some sort and knocked unconscious. That was all she knew.

Tommy told the police how he'd found her and then they took him home to bed. It wasn't until morning that he had a chance to return to the lab and investigate the case on his own. By that time, Professor Blake had returned from Boston and the place was crowded with people. Both of the graduate students — bearded Michael Bush and curly-haired Sam Young — were there, along with Nora and two detectives.

As soon as Professor Blake arrived, he went to Max's cage and inspected the damage to the wiring. "Not too serious, but it'll take a few days to rewire it," he said.

Max was making an uproar, pounding on the bars. As soon as Professor Blake opened the outer door he scurried across the yard to the puzzle tree, climbing high into its maze of branches.

"It's almost as if he's trying to tell us something," Tommy observed.

"Yes, it is," Professor Blake agreed. "If the machine were working, I think he could tell us who attacked Nora."

"Do you think a chimp could do that?" Sam Young asked. "He's not human, you know."

"But after Nora was knocked out, whoever hit her came in here," Tommy said. "Max would have seen him."

Nora still had a bump on her head, but she was much better than she had been the previous night. She was seated at her desk, making a list of what was stolen. "As near as I can tell, he got all our experimental data on Max, plus some of the other work you've been doing here, Professor."

"It almost has to be someone familiar with the place," he said. "He knew just where to look."

Mitch arrived then, too, having heard about the robbery, and Tommy filled him in on what little he knew. "Remember the way that Bush was looking around yesterday?" he asked. "Tommy, I'll bet——"

"We were looking around, too, Mitch. Detective work means evidence, not guessing."

"But don't you think——"

"I don't think anything yet."

Michael Bush was trying to coax Max out of his tree, but without success. Every few minutes the chimp would edge down a bit, but as they approached him, he always ran back up. The limbs of the monkey-puzzle tree were so twisted and intertwined that it was impossible for anyone to reach him.

"What would you ask Max?" Tommy questioned Nora. "If the machine hadn't been damaged, what would you ask him?"

"Oh, I'd probably say *Who hurt Nora?* That's about all I could ask with the symbols we have."

"But there is a symbol for the tree, isn't there?" Tommy was studying the damaged machine. "And as soon as he was free Max ran to the tree."

"But what could it mean?"

"I don't know," Tommy admitted.

"I agree with Sam," Michael Bush said. "And it's not often the two of us agree. But Max isn't human. You can't expect him to do human things."

"Max can communicate in a limited way," Nora insisted. "Someone stole our data and sabotaged the machine to prevent his communicating. Someone familiar with the workings of the lab."

"Why would anyone care so much?" Bush asked.

"Our research is valuable," Professor Blake said. "Many people would pay well for it."

Sam Young ran a hand through his hair. "I'm more worried about Nora. This thief, whoever he is, could have killed her."

"I've got a hard head," she said. "And right now I think Professor Blake will agree that our first task is to get Max out of that tree."

Tommy was staring at the dangling wires of the communication keyboard. He pressed one of the square symbols and an idea came to him. "Of course!" he exclaimed. "Nora, if you can get Max out of that tree, I know how we can get him to tell us who hit you!"

"That's a big order, boy," one of the detectives said.

"I'm sure he can do it."

Nora shrugged. "If you're sure, Tommy, so am I."

It took her the better part of a half-hour to lure Max out of the tree. Then, carrying him in her arms as she would a child, she followed Tommy back into the lab.

"Look here," Tommy said, pointing to the keyboard. "Max knows this machine because it's the same as the one on the other side of the wall, in his cage.

The wires that were pulled loose are just for the lights, to show which buttons have been pushed. But you don't need lights to talk with Max. Just hold him facing the keyboard and slowly touch the squares you want. Touch *Who hurt Nora?* and he'll get your message."

"Of course!" Nora said. "Professor, we should have thought of that!"

"You're a smart lad," Professor Blake told Tommy.

As Nora reached out a finger to touch the buttons, holding Max tightly with her other arm, Tommy said, "I don't really need Max to tell me. I know who hit you, Nora, and robbed this place last night."

"So do I!" Mitch chimed in. "It just came to me!"

DO *YOU* KNOW WHO THE THIEF IS? HAVE YOU BEATEN TOMMY PRESTON TO THE SOLUTION? TURN THE PAGE TO FIND OUT IF YOU'RE RIGHT!

"All right, Mitch," Tommy said. "Who do you think did it?"

Mitch pointed a finger at Michael Bush. "He did! Max couldn't light up *tree* on his machine, so he kept running out to the monkey-puzzle tree to tell us. He was saying *tree* because it was the closest he could get to the name *Bush!*"

Tommy and the others laughed at that. "Mitch, the chimp doesn't know that a bush is like a small tree. You're acting like he's human. That makes no more sense than saying the tree reminded him of Sam Young because Sam's curly hair is like the tangled limbs of the tree. Humans might think in those terms, but animals certainly don't."

"Then who——?"

But Nora was already pressing the buttons slowly, so Max could see.

WHO

HURT

NORA

And Max replied at once in the only way he could. He pressed the square symbol for PROFESSOR.

Professor Blake turned to flee, but already the detectives were on him, holding him. Nora simply stared, unbelieving. "Professor Blake! I can't believe it!"

"Don't you see?" Tommy said. "Max was behaving like an animal and nothing more. He ran out to the monkey-puzzle tree not to give us a message but to hide from Professor Blake, so he wouldn't be hurt too."

"But how did you know?" asked Nora.

"The thief ripped out those wires to prevent your communicating with Max, hoping that by the time the

wires were fixed, Max would have forgotten the entire incident. But how could Max tell us the name of the thief, given only these sixty-four word symbols? He couldn't communicate Bush or Young or any other name. The only people he could specifically identify were NORA and PROFESSOR. If the thief feared Max, it had to be because the thief was the professor."

"Why steal his own records?" the detectives asked Tommy.

"Because he was leaving for another job and he couldn't take them along. He wanted the records, but the only way to get them was to fake a robbery. He returned early from Boston, hit Nora on the head, took what he needed, and then ripped out those wires so Max couldn't betray him. He couldn't bring himself to harm Max, of course, which was another indication that the thief was someone very close to the chimp."

"You know something, kid?" the detective said. "You'd make a pretty good detective someday."

Tommy only smiled. "I've got to get back to school," he said. "I just came by for a library book I forgot."

THE STOLEN SAPPHIRE

"Tommy," Mr. Preston said one Saturday morning in May, "I want you to run an errand with your sister, Sandy."

"Do I have to, Dad?" At thirteen, Tommy found his fourteen-year-old sister a difficult companion.

But Tommy's father was adamant. "The high school asked if it could borrow a live snake from the zoo for today's science fair. I've got a little garter snake they can have. It's perfectly safe and a good one for children to handle. Sandy is taking it to school in an animal carrier, but I want you to go along, too, just to make sure nothing happens to it."

"All right," Tommy agreed. He was finishing his first year of junior high, and the idea of showing up at the school with a live snake from his father's zoo appealed to him. "Where's Sandy?"

"Out in back, waiting for you. Deliver the snake to Mr. Cullins, the science teacher, and be careful with it."

He found his sister with the animal carrier, a box with a handle and wire-mesh sides. It was perfect for transporting small animals, and although these creatures were usually the four-legged variety, there was no reason why a snake couldn't be carried this way, too.

The high school was about a mile away, which wasn't a long walk on such a pleasant day. "Where's your friend Mitch today?" Sandy asked.

"The band's been rehearsing for the Memorial Day parade and he's got practice this morning. Maybe we'll see him at school." Mitch played a trumpet in the band and Tommy sometimes went behind the school building to watch him practicing with the others.

"What do they have at the science fair?" Sandy asked. "I didn't go last year."

"Lots of experiments and exhibits the kids put together, with minerals, fossils, small animals. That's what the snake is for."

Tommy and Sandy entered the school through the rear door and went at once to the gym, where the science fair was being readied for its noon opening. The animal exhibits were grouped together along the right side as they entered, with the kids' experiments in the center section, and the fossils and minerals along the left side. There were several older students about, and some teachers as well. One of the teachers, a slender man with long dark hair, was attaching an identification tag to a large elephant tusk in the animal section.

I love

Tommy read the tag and said at once, "That's wrong."

The teacher stared at him. "What?"

"The tag says *Tusk of a female Indian elephant*, but only male Indian elephants have tusks."

"Who are you, anyway?"

GEMS
FOSSIL
Instructions
7th Grade Science
Experiment.

"Tommy Preston, and this is my sister Sandy. My dad is the zoo keeper. You're Mr. Cullins, aren't you?"

"That's right — Hugh Cullins. I teach tenth-grade science here. Is that garter snake for me?"

"Sure is! My dad sent it over."

"Thanks for the loan of it." He placed the animal carrier in a position of honor right next to the elephant tusk. "So you think this is the tusk of an Indian male?"

"More likely African, judging by its length. The Indian ones are rarely more than five feet long, and this is closer to eight feet. In Africa both males and females have tusks."

"You know a great deal about animals."

Tommy beamed. "You get to learn it, hanging around a zoo."

Hugh Cullins bent to examine the garter snake. "Can the kids handle it?"

"Sure, it's harmless and gentle." He glanced around and saw that Sandy and a girl friend had wandered off into the hall. He strolled across the gym to the mineral exhibit against the opposite wall, where he was stopped by a pleasant blonde woman, another of the teachers.

"The fair's not quite open yet," she informed him. "I'm Mrs. Stewart. May I help you?"

"I was delivering a snake to Mr. Cullins——"

"My word! A live snake!"

"Sure — it's in that animal carrier over there."

As he tried to slip past her, she blocked his way once more. "You see, we have a valuable sapphire on display here as part of the mineral exhibit on how gems are formed. Mr. Wallace, whose son is in the senior class, graciously lent us the stone."

Tommy became aware of Mr. Wallace, a stout man in a blue business suit, who was standing by the exhibit. "It's not all that valuable as sapphires go," he said, "but it's worth ten thousand dollars, and I'd hate losing one of the best gems from my store. You can see why we're not letting people get too close."

"I understand," Tommy agreed at once, circling around the guarded area. Even from a distance, the bright-blue stone was a sight to behold.

Mr. Wallace glanced at his watch. "It's a half-hour yet before the science fair opens. I'll just put the sapphire back in its box till then, to remove temptation."

Tommy wondered if the remark was meant for him. He shrugged and went into the hallway, where Sandy and her girl friend were giggling over something. "Oh, there you are, Tommy," Sandy said.

"We should be getting back."

"Aren't you even going to stay for the science fair?"

Tommy thought about it. "Well, I guess we could. It's nearly noon."

He glanced back inside and saw that Hugh Cullins had strolled over from his animal exhibit to join Wallace and Mrs. Stewart at the sapphire display area. Then he noticed a familiar figure. His friend Mitch Grady had come in, dressed in his band uniform and carrying his trumpet case.

"Mitch!" Tommy called to him. "Over here!"

Mitch grinned and set down his case against the wall. "What are you doing here on a Saturday, Tommy? Come for the science fair?"

"We delivered a snake from the zoo. It's over in that box."

KNIFE CORAL
Thecosmilia trichoto
Petrified Wood
160 million years

The words were hardly out of Tommy's mouth when he noticed that something was wrong. The door of the animal carrier was standing open an inch or two. And the garter snake was nowhere in sight.

Tommy hurried over to Mr. Cullins with the news. "I think the snake's escaped!"

"That's impossible!" Cullins exclaimed. But he followed Tommy back to the display. Mr. Wallace came too, telling Mrs. Stewart to stay with the jewel box. Sandy and her girl friend had been attracted by the uproar, and they joined the hunt.

It didn't take long for Tommy to find the snake, wrapped around the upper part of one of the table legs. He returned it to the box and Hugh Cullins sighed with relief. "I know it's harmless," he said, "but we couldn't open the fair with it crawling around the place."

He went back and relieved Mrs. Stewart of her guard duty so she could help put up some signs over the chemical-experiments section. Tommy went across the hall with Mitch while he stowed the trumpet case in his locker. As they returned, Mitch asked, "How do you think the snake got out, Tommy?"

"That latch is a little loose. A push on the door might have opened it."

"Maybe somebody let him out on purpose."

"Mr. Cullins was the only one near it, and he wouldn't do that."

It was just about noon, and the teachers were putting the finishing touches on the exhibits as the student participants took their positions. Mr. Wallace returned to the mineral display and opened the jewel box.

"I've been robbed!" he shouted out. "The sapphire is gone!"

Tommy and the others quickly gathered around, and they could see it was true. "Who could have taken it?" Mrs. Stewart asked. "We were guarding it every minute!"

Mr. Wallace, red-faced and excited, had an answer for that. "None of the students were allowed near it. Only you and Cullins were ever alone at this box. It had to be one of you!"

But now Hugh Cullins interrupted. "Just wait a minute before you accuse us! You could have palmed the sapphire yourself when you put it back in the box. Maybe you stole it yourself for the insurance money!"

Tommy thought Mr. Wallace would hit him then, but Mrs. Stewart managed to keep them apart. "None of us has left the gym at any time," she said. "We'll all have to be searched. And all the exhibits will have to be searched too."

She was right, of course. Everyone remained where he was in the gym and the word was passed that the opening of the science fair had been delayed a few hours. One of the teachers outside was delegated to phone the police.

When the police arrived, Wallace and Cullins and Mrs. Stewart were the first to be searched. Tommy wasn't surprised when the blue sapphire remained undiscovered. He knew the thief would be clever enough not to hide it on himself. But with close to a hundred exhibits in the gym, finding it seemed impossible. First the police searched the other teachers and students who'd been present, and then they turned their attention to the exhibits.

Sandy and the boys helped out with some ideas of

their own. Tommy's sister went over the elephant tusk with care, examining it for a secret compartment. Watching her, Mitch chuckled. "Imagine a secret compartment in an elephant tusk! Only a girl would think of something like that!"

But Tommy noticed that Mitch himself was intent on finding the missing sapphire in a beakerful of blue liquid set up for one of the chemistry experiments. "It's like hiding an ice cube in a glass of water, Tommy! The blue stone wouldn't show in here!"

"The thief wouldn't risk damage to the jewel in those chemicals," Tommy pointed out.

Tables, chairs, signs — even the animals' cages — were all examined by the police. Tommy took the

garter snake from the animal carrier and stroked its slim body while the carrier itself was searched.

But the blue sapphire was still missing.

When the detectives could only shrug and shake their heads, Tommy got their attention. "Look here," he said, "it's the timing that's important. Only Mr. Wallace or Mrs. Stewart or Mr. Cullins could have stolen the jewel — and each one would have had to do it at a different time."

"What do you mean, boy?" the detective asked.

"Well, Mr. Wallace was never alone with the sapphire. If he stole his own jewel for the insurance, it had to be while he was putting it in the box. Then he might have unlocked my animal carrier later so the escape of the snake would create a diversion. The jewel wasn't stolen then, but we'd *think* it was — and blame whoever was alone with it."

"Mrs. Stewart!" Wallace sputtered. "I didn't take it, she did, while we were all after that snake!"

"That's preposterous!" the woman teacher replied. "Why, I never went near the snake! I'm deathly afraid of them. I couldn't have unlatched that carrier."

"I'll admit you were nowhere near the snake," Tommy agreed. "But I pointed out that the latch was loose and might have opened accidentally."

"I was by the snake," Hugh Cullins said. "I suppose I'm a likely suspect, all right. But remember I wasn't alone with the jewel box till later, while Mrs. Stewart was arranging the signs."

The mention of the signs sent the detectives back for another search, but they were no more successful. Tommy waited until they'd given up and then went on with his comments. "Look, if you find out *when* the jewel was taken, you'll know who took it. Mr. Wallace's only opportunity was around eleven thirty, a half-hour before the scheduled opening, when he put the jewel in its box. Mrs. Stewart's only opportunity was while the snake was loose. And Mr. Cullins would have had to do it later, just before the theft was discovered."

"But there's no way we can tell when it happened," Mitch pointed out, and Tommy agreed with him. He felt he was on the verge of solving the mystery, but he didn't quite have the solution yet.

"None of the three left the gym," he said, half to himself, "and yet the jewel's gone. It's nowhere in this room."

"Maybe it's somewhere nobody thought to look,' Sandy volunteered, staring up at the basketball hoop above their heads.

"No, the thief couldn't have climbed up anywhere without being noticed."

"Maybe he swallowed it."

Tommy considered that but shook his head. "The jewel's pretty big. He couldn't take a chance on choking and attracting attention."

The police, too, were ready to give up. "Let the insurance company find it," one of them said. "We sure can't."

Finally, the gymnasium doors were thrown open, and the science fair got under way two hours late. But for Tommy and the others, it lacked real excitement. He was still puzzling out the problem of the stolen sapphire. Sandy drifted off with her girl friend and finally he left with Mitch.

"I want to go home and get out of this band uniform," Mitch said. "Don't know why we had to wear it to practice anyway."

Tommy grunted and kicked at a stone as they walked along the street. "Probably to see how you'll look, marching in the parade," he suggested. "It's Monday, isn't it?"

"Yeah."

"I don't know where Sandy went. I suppose I'll have to come back for the snake after the science fair ends tonight."

"You're giving up on the missing sapphire?"

Tommy shook his head. "No. In fact, I have an idea we might be able to find it tonight."

It was just getting dark when they returned to the school, slipping in the side door as the last of the visitors departed. In the gymnasium, the various displays and experiments were being dismantled. There was no sign of Mr. Wallace, but Hugh Cullins and Mrs. Stewart were at their booths, cleaning up.

"Did the sapphire ever turn up?" Tommy asked the woman.

"Not a trace. It's as if it melted away."

"Melted!" Mitch exclaimed. "Of course! It was made of blue-colored ice and it melted while it was in that box! Mr. Wallace never even brought the real one!"

Tommy laughed. "Golly, Mitch, you'll never make a detective. Don't you remember the jewel was on display when we arrived? It didn't show any signs of melting then. And the box wasn't wet or anything after Mr. Wallace opened it. Blue water would have left a damp blue stain."

"Well, it was a good idea anyway," he grumbled. "But I think I've got a better one. Let's——"

Before he could finish, Hugh Cullins came up to them with the animal carrier. "Here's your snake back, Tommy. Thank your dad for me."

"I will, Mr. Cullins."

They started for the door and Mitch whispered, "Are we really leaving, Tommy?"

"Of course not, but we want people to think we are."

They slipped around the back of the school building and reentered by a door on the other side. There was a pay telephone there, and Tommy dialed the police.

"You told the police to come?" Mitch asked. "Are you that sure of where the jewel is?"

"I'm pretty sure, Mitch. And knowing where it is tells me who stole it."

WHERE IS THE SAPPHIRE AND WHO STOLE IT? TURN THE PAGE TO SEE IF YOU'VE BEATEN TOMMY PRESTON TO THE SOLUTION!

As they crouched in the darkness of the school corridor, just outside the gym, Mitch whispered, "Of course! I should have guessed it before! The jewel is inside the garter snake. He swallowed it! Snakes can unhinge their jaws to swallow big things."

"Sure, snakes can," Tommy agreed, "but even if a snake was dumb enough to swallow the jewel, he'd bulge out with it. We could have seen it. I thought of the snake too, and that's why I held him while they searched his carrier. But he was all snake. Not a hard spot on him."

"You *searched* the snake, Tommy?"

"I suppose you could say that." Then he heard something and motioned with his finger. Someone was coming.

They saw the shadowy figure pause in the corridor and turn on a flashlight. Then there was the sound of metal on metal.

"My locker!" Mitch exclaimed.

"Come on," Tommy said, moving fast. His hand hit the light switch on the wall and suddenly the hallway was bathed in light.

There, holding a short crowbar at the door of Mitch's locker, was Mrs. Stewart.

The police arrived almost at once, and she offered no resistance. She only stared down at Tommy and asked, "How did you know?"

"The police searched every person and every place in the gym, and the sapphire wasn't there. So it must have been removed, somehow. Walking home this afternoon with Mitch, I remembered his band practice. There was one thing — only one thing — that was removed from the gym during the crucial period. Mitch's

trumpet case. He carried it across the hall and put it in this locker. And before that, while the snake was loose, he'd left it on the floor for a few moments, unguarded. When the snake got free by accident, you saw your chance and stole the sapphire, hiding it in the trumpet case while our attention was diverted."

Mitch opened his case and found the jewel tucked snugly behind the velvet lining. "But Tommy — even if you knew it was here, how did you know Mrs. Stewart was the thief?"

"I told you the time of the theft was important. You carried your trumpet case over to the locker before Mr. Cullins was alone with the sapphire, so he couldn't be

the thief. Mr. Wallace might have stolen it earlier and waited for a chance to hide it, but two things worked against his being guilty. First, he went with Mr. Cullins to search for the snake, so he couldn't have used that opportunity to hide the jewel in your case. Second, and more important, Mr. Wallace was a parent, an outsider. He wouldn't be likely to know that you kept your trumpet case in the locker rather than at home at night. And he'd have no way of getting into the school to retrieve the hidden sapphire. The thief had to be Mrs. Stewart, and I figured she'd try to get into your locker tonight. She certainly couldn't wait till Monday, when you'd be using the trumpet in the parade."

Mrs. Stewart broke down and confessed then. "It was a foolish thing to do, but I saw my chance when the snake got free and I took it. I arranged to leave Hugh Cullins alone with the case later, so he'd be a suspect too. Why did I do it? I guess I just needed the money."

As they walked home later, Mitch asked Tommy, "Are you coming to the parade?"

"I wouldn't miss it, Mitch. Not after it helped me solve the mystery."